THE CORPERSTEIN

Tale of a Monstrous Corper

(A Play)

JOSEPH DAVID ARI

THE CORPERSTEIN

Tale of a Monstrous Corper

(A Play)

JOSEPH DAVID ARI

THE CORPERSTEIN

By **Joseph David Ari**
ISBN: 978-978-965-122-1

Library of Congress in Cataloguing–in-publication Data

Joseph David Ari
For enquiries/correspondence:
Mobile: +234 7037288050
Email:

First Printed and Published in Nigeria by

NIRPRI PUBLISHERS
Suite B1. Commerce Plaza,
Area 1, Garki, FCT, Abuja, Nigeria.
nirpripublishers16@gmail.com
+234 813 459 5955

Preface

The play Corperstein is an outlook at the social malaise observable in the third stage of the NYSC exercise by Corps members, whose opportunism in the act is not true to type. The play tends to look at the onus upon which NYSC as a scheme was established as well as viewing play writing as not only, a source of entertainment or profit maximization but, as a tool for conscientization and socio-cultural development. Corperstein is about a jealously guided sociological perspective between two Corps members. The perspective which is of a sociological discourse, tries to give meaning to a less discussed matter of social relationship in our society, where young girls fall victims to Corps members serving in their locale.

Tolu tries to "determine who is right in the concept of socio- romantic or sexual relationship," between boys and girls, which in a way illuminates the danger in an attitude, which accompany any individual who may feel that they are right in displaying some sort of cleverness which has the propensity to harm the other individual involved in the social act who often feel cheated. The environment in which the play is situated embroils the post NYSC orientation camp activities of Corps members, which in a technical conception housed the discussed concept. The play revolves majorly around Kola and Tolu, Corps members who were posted to the village of Oleagyida.

Kola on one hand is a socialite who feels that simply asking a girl out is not only normal, but telling her lies (deception) about his intension and finally displacing her when he feels the fun is no longer there, without the slightest concern for her feelings, is how life is and how the game should be played. On the other hand, is Tolu, a young man of many theories, who believes that, it's only not fair, but it's equally fraudulent and criminal as well to think and practice Kola's conceptualization of socialization.

While these issues might seem a bit intertwined, Corperstein tries to debunk issues in the patriarchal and matriarchal systems within societies, from whence the argument for and against certain pattern of social relationships emerged. The Feminists perspective is upheld in defence for women rights, domestic violence, gender inequality and the support for the girl child education is at the core.

Dedication

This book is dedicated to the almighty God for the wisdom conferred. To Victor Kadri, Tobiloba Babatunde Ogunwuyi, Grace Iberri and Oluchi, the Corp members I served with at the vocational college, Obollo Orie, Enugu State in 2016, my NYSC service year.

Characters

Narrator		
Kola	**-**	**Main character**
Tolu	**-**	**Kola's friend**
The bike man 1&2		
The principal		
Uju	**-**	**Kola's girl friend**
Mr and Mrs. Alabi	**-**	**Kola's parent**
Mama Uju	**-**	**Uju's mother**
Papa Uju	**-**	**Uju's father**
Mr. Coldliver	**-**	**The shop owner**
Musty	**-**	**Kola's school friend**
The Corp boy 1		
The Corp boy 2		
The Corp boy 3		
The Spirit Woman		
Musty's Girlfriend		

Prologue

Lights shone on the narrator on stage as he made his way through the seats of the audience. A man in his seventies, in his old regalia, walking majestically with his walking stick serving as the chorus to the rhythm of his walking steps. (A very delicate sound of the drums ends and our man, the narrator stands and says) Good evening, ladies and gentlemen, welcome to the home of con-scientisation, where you have the free will to decide what is either good or bad. Life is indeed a mythical antecedent, as you are bound to come across that which you plan for and the ones you did not plan. Hmm... life in the course of living and life in general is nothing but a race of survival for the existentialist. So, I implore you, I mean you (pointing as if with a target in the audience) yes, you to sit, relax, and enjoy as, the story unfolds... (Dance out to light fade). Light meets Mr and Mrs Alabi, in their living room, seated respectively in their chairs with their gaze raised to the ceiling and back down.

Kola: Daddy, Mummy, you will not believe what has happened to me in these few months where my service took place.

Kola's Parents: (Mr. and Mrs. Alabi snap out of their amusement) Ehen, my son (said Mr Alabi), so what exactly happened to you?

(Scratching the area close to his nose) You see my son; you have really changed and I will like to know what happened to the old Kola...

Kola: No one actually believes me, just as you have behaved right now. But with little hope and conviction, you and mum will adjust to this new me. Tolu asked me to be careful and it was he who doubted this most when it all started.

(Light picks the narrator from the other end of the theatre as he whistles his way to the centre stage, a short round of drumming ends and the narrator is heared saying) The people we see are not really the people we think they are. Not to worry you, I will need to go back to the chthonic realm (signals the drumming to begin as he dances out in panegyric... Back to the sitting room)

Kola: Mummy, Daddy, there lives a beast in me No! Not in me, but in the place where I was serving. I didn't believe it until I killed other beasts with the beast...

Mr Alabi: (Cuts in) what are you saying son? What do you mean by, with the beast, more so, which beast? And by the beast do you mean an animal or human beast?

Kola: (cuts in) no ... Daddy, just listen for a moment, you will understand everything. I have to start from the beginning, yes, I have to. I have a friend called Tolu, who was also posted to the place where it all happened. Tolu has always been that one person who questioned my methods or bravery especially in the way and manner in which I carry out my social pattern of life. So, it all started with us at the park.

Act One, Scene One

(The drumming starts and ends, the narrator is seen on stage echoing ... This is how events unfold). The sun is almost half way in the sky, with people from different backgrounds moving up and down, while others are gathered with vehicles carrying loads of baggage and bike men trying to convince customers to board with them. Therein Kola and his friend Tolu appear in what seems like the motor park.

Tolu: It hurts, that we are to serve in the same place, after all my prayers for otherwise.

Kola: Paddy mi, leave that thing. Who wants to be around you, you kill my moral anyways.

Tolu: As if to say, the four years we spent together in school is not enough, NYSC had to put us together again. Anyway, I'm just going to manage you for another one year of service after that, we shall see if anything will bring us together again. What bothers me the most is your stupid methodology; you go ahead and pretend to be my friend and then leave me alone to handle those other female friends of yours when you leave them heartbroken. Look it's not going to work for you this time around.

Kola: Haha... that is why I gbadun you, my paddy. You will get angry only to return helping me again.

Tolu: I think you have got Kokoro in your head (Kokoro is slang).

Kola: I agree with you, and you will always be the cure to my Kokoro.

Tolu: Trust me, not this time around Nemesis will catch up with you surely and sooner.

Kola: Please forget all this talk and let us focus on how to get to this nonsensical village, we have been posted to, moreover I thought you said you knew the place?

Tolu: I never said such a thing. I only said I have heard little about the place and it is not pleasant at all.

Kola: Pleasant or not, let's just find our way there, I can't wait to start eating those girls like *suya*

Act One, Scene Two

(The drumming starts and ends) Narrator: ... And so, they stop at a motor cycle park and ask a bike man if they were at the right town and if they are familiar with Oleagyida village. The bike man responded rather well, something most corps members love to hear when posted to strange places for service. They took the bike directly to the school they were to serve at, as the bike man is familiar with the place. They were directed to the office of the principal for either acceptance or rejection letter, as it's the procedure of the corps service. (The sounds of the drums, from the backstage rose to a crescendo, which he dances to a halt, and he says). At the office of the principal, well-furnished upholstery with art works well displayed, already seated is a man in his fifties, tall dark and full of smiles attending to papers displayed before him).

Kola: Thank you very much Mr. Principal for accepting us, we are very grateful.

Principal: Now, you two, please take it easy with the villagers. I suppose you have heard talks about this place, right?

Tolu: Well, very little sir, but we will keep our peace bearing in mind the four-cardinal principles of the scheme.

Kola: Yeah, yes, we will sir.

(Nonchalantly)

Act One, Scene Three

(The drumming starts and stops, the narrator is heard saying) The anxiety of getting to know the community and the likes is beginning to pile up... Hmm the journey soon gets started (this time a song is raised from the background which gave cue, which leads to a standstill shifting action from the narrator)

(At the Lodge)

Kola: Tolu, can you see what I'm seeing?

(*His eyes moving from one point to the other in admiration***)** Is it my eyes or what? This village is not as nonsensical as I earlier thought.

Tolu: Kola! Kola! You have started again right. Just few minutes of our arrival and you have already started right.

Kola: Look my friend, girls are for the taking, and after all, they were made from our ribs I learnt. More so, it's written that they shall be our companion. Take thee a concubine, as it is written in the Holy books, Haha. *(Laughs away)*

Tolu: You may be right though, but not completely. You may have left something out, and that is marriage.

Kola: Marriage my foot, look young man let me flirt, you hear me right, let me flirt.

Act One, Scene Four

(The drumming began, and ends quickly and here comes the narrator who roars) More often than not, amongst young people, nonchalant attitude is mistaken for identity in hosting and keeping peer group bond alive. It's such that, members of the group feel save, if the most influential among them misbehaves, it's rather seen as bravery. Groups like this are found at the camp breaking camp rules. Having misinterpreted the cardinal points of NYSC as a scheme, Kola, a leader of his group, went about his act of calumny in the face of morals... please you (as if to beckon on someone then retreat) what next? (He raises his head to the sky as if in supplication then staggers to regain his balance) I will be back... (A young beautiful village girl comes passing.)

Kola: Hi beautiful

Uju: Good day master *(Addressing Kola as it is the custom when addressing teachers in the village)*

Kola: Did you go this direction same time yesterday? Because I swear, I saw you Yesterday *(Even though it was a lie)*

Uju: Yes, I did. If you don't mind, please can I go?

Kola: Yes, but please wait, what is that your beautiful name?

Uju: How do you mean? You don't even know me, let alone agreeing that I have got a beautiful name.

Kola: Look, I don't know what is happening to me, but I was very excited to have seen you yesterday. It was as if I saw a goddess.

Uju: But I'm not.

(The drumming stops and the narrator is seen saying) The magic word in action (He breaks into laughter) Ha-ha, someone who ought to be on her way now stops and is interested in the magic word "goddess". Are you still there?

Kola: Take it or leave it, you have got curves, and your curves are perfectly carved. You have this slim round neck with lines like rings round them. Your shoulder is not only feminine, but they are also filled, plum, such that even now that you sweat due to a little walk under the sun, it looks like diamond in water.

Uju: I know your type, with sugar coated tongue and oil in their mouth, the type young girls like, and always fall for, but I am an exception.

Kola: No, no, no, your thoughts are wrong; I am the one and will remain the only one, who tells...

You are the one
whose Beauty Savours my heart with smiles,
You are the one,
whose smell harkens to the instinct of the king from miles,
You are the one,
who provokes my style,
You are the one,
with the best sets of thighs,
You are the one;
I will write for and put in files,
So that history documents and keeps a slice.
My name is Master Kola and what is yours?

(the drumming began and the narrator is seen whistling from down stage, approaches the audience and comes to a definite halt and says) Hmm, Uju is epileptic at the rendition of those lines, as she is tactically crushed by the poem and can only smile and laugh at every other thing said...

Uju: My name is Uju. Please I'm already running late for the stream, can I please go now? I will see you in no time... *(Kola convinced of his success keeps smiling till light fades...)*

Act Two, Scene One

Light picks Tolu sitting under a tree at the lodge, eating banana in a short and a white tee-shirt, humming.

Tolu: Mister, where have you been all this while?

Kola: My paddy, I met one sweet, lovely, in fact, the most beautiful babe in the world today.

Tolu: Hey, you have not been to work since and all you can talk about is a girl. You have started right? Haven't I warned you about these girls? Leave them alone.

What is your problem? It's not as if you want to keep this one.

Kola: Look, look, Tolu *(charging towards him)* my friend, let me explain, this one is different, and I saw beauty today. She was tying wrapper over her breast exposing her very curvy and neatly greasy waist. She is so round from her hip down to her knee. When she smiles, her cheek gathers, bringing out dimples that kills. Did I forget to mention her skin? Her skin colour, you won't believe that they have such in this village. Her hair was braided with rubber, unlike that of the city girls who wear wigs, yet she looks really amazing and stunning. I must have the one, even if it's the last thing I do here.

Tolu: Hmm, your work! (*Your work, is a slang)*
Who has honey in his mouth like you? You will be saying she is the only girl for me, my life, my all and all for now. Later, the same Kola will return with a wicked theory saying, there is a thin line between love and hate. I know you. Please, just let her go ok.

Kola: That is your cup of tea. I must have this one. Eat and clean mouth like a thief, like nothing happen. You seat and watch me.

Tolu: Kola, I was told by one of the female teachers, that in this village, during cashew season, if you eat the fruit, you have to return the fruit seed back to the place where you picked it.

Kola: And what will happen if I don't return it and decided to make cashew nuts out of it?

Tolu: I was not told of what will happen, but I believe she said something like evil will befall you.

Kola: Nigerian film, forget that crap.

Tolu: This is like a parable; the cashew could mean anything, for example, a girl or some person's property.

Kola: Tolu, you too dey fear, you no sharp at all!! What exactly is your problem with women, always protecting them, are you a feminist?

Tolu: If you like call me nerd or a baff. All I know is that girls too have feelings and they are human. In fact, I have a theory for you and your type.

Kola: You have started. Look I am never going to buy any of your theory. But you can go ahead and say it.

Tolu: Tell me, because I have been fighting you for quite some time now about girls and the way you treat them. Let me ask, what exactly do you want from a girl you don't know vividly, you are never going to marry? What do you call whatsoever you are doing? And finally, do they deserve your lies?

Kola: Look, my paddy; if you don't lie to girls, they will never believe you.

Girls kind of, don't like guys who say the truth. Finally, I feel a kind of prestige when I get what I want.

Tolu: Hmm, Kola! Kola! You wouldn't change!!

Kola: As for the breaking hearts aspect, that is a different ball game.

You see after getting down with a girl, she tends to want attention which I may not be willing to give. So, you just break up with her. Moreso, you need to break the news first, hence you feel hurt the most, simple.

Tolu: This is not fair.

Kola: Fairness is not part of the game.

Tolu: So, it is a game to you.

Kola: I can't continue to eat the same type of food every day na; there is need for a change my friend.

Tolu: Well, let me key you in on my theory. Whatever fun you think you are having is 'fraudulent', therefore fraudulent fun produces unhealthy fun environment that is it.

Kola: Hmm, is that the theory?

Tolu: Yes, a theory could be that, can't it? In fact, allow me to break it down for you. Some form of social formation not designed by you causes you to conform to the notion of flirting as fun, which is not. It's another form of social psychology that informs your mind that the flesh, skin colour, wetness, softness and the tenderness that your mind feels when your body comes in contact with the body of the opposite sex is for real, which is also not real.

Kola: What in God's name are you saying?

Tolu: It's even good you made mention of God's name. But let me finish with my initial explanation

Kola: Oh, you are not done yet?

Tolu: Yes. Now imagine knowing what something looks like, if you have your eyes closed or if you don't have any.

Kola: Well, if I don't have eyes, I don't know.

Tolu: Exactly what I am saying. These sensory neurons, your eye, brain, helps you make sense of things and think you are catching fun.

Kola: So, what, what do you think about the LGBTQ?

Tolu: It's the same. That is why they see nothing wrong with it. Their social conditioning informs them to feel for same sex and they simply obey. Social formation, social action and in fact, combined with social conditioning, forms the social being. It will seize to exist if you get a knock on your head and you were told you had a brain accident or memory loss.

Kola: Look my paddy, God said, go out there and procreate.

Tolu: Really? Is that what God really said? And even if that is your opinion, where is it written, then provoke them after procreation? Look, you will agree with me that there is a process to which it should be done at least.

Kola: I don't have time for this theory of yours for now. I am going hunting *jare*. I'm going to trace her to her house and if possible, pay her a visit. You know my style of introducing myself to the family, and looking as if it's serious. Then bang, I'm fed and puff I'm gone.

Tolu: Well, since I can't stop you with all my grammar, you are on your own.

Kola: Just wish me good luck and stop wailing.

Act Two, Scene Two

(Drumming began and the narrator was seen saying) The tales about the place of Primary Assignment is one that is juicy, especially for those who care to listen. The moment you just ask what had happened in the past, it just start flowing and so, Oleagyida village is a place where lack of basic necessity of life gives one the creep. Hmm... So it was, yes (nodding his head as if in the affirmation as he takes to the edge of the stage). Sunset with Kola and Tolu on a bike heading towards the exit of the community where Banks are found for withdrawal appears as it is tensed with ups and downs of the day's activities.)

The Bike man: Where to?
Kola: Old Road, where the banks are.
The Bike man: Alright climb.
Kola: How much sir?
The Bike man: Just climb on.
Climbs hurriedly without hesitation...
Kola: But Oga, you know the way you bike men behave if one does not ask how much you charge. You may end up saying it's not the usual price again.

The Bike man: That is true. Some of the bike men often do so. More often than not they intentionally increase the fare. And that is why you are right to always ask for price of the fare before you board bike around here. The people of Oleagyida village love money too much and may not be willing to pardon you.

Kola: Watch out!!

Bike man; *(Quickly turns away from danger, another bike man was not looking at all before switching lane)*

Kola: (*Shouts at the other the man who was less concern)* Young man!! Watch what you are doing na!!

Bike man: Spirit, I tell you, spirits!!

Tolu: What do you mean by spirit?

Bike man: Hmm, you are new here, right? Well, you shouldn't keep your eyes closed from seeing the things before you. You should be warned. Well, some people in this village are spirits. I tell, you wouldn't know, but I tell you that is what they are! In fact, I saw one the other day, my passenger said so too. "He said it wasn't ordinary"

Kola: What happened and what do you mean by not ordinary?

The Bike man: This person was standing on the road carelessly, I blazed my horned tirelessly, but she just refused to move away from the road. When I got closer to her, she disappeared and reappeared on the other side of the road,

Tolu: *(Not a fan of African tradition).* You people. Hmm, sir, are you sure of what you saw? Are you under the influence of something? I think you want us to bank on hearsay...

The Bike man: *(Cuts in) No...* But I swear that is what happened. Well, you will see it for yourself, if you continue to live in this place, I bet you.

Tolu: In as much as I hate listening to things like this, I kind of wish its true, so that my crazy friend here Kola will stop the misconceptions.

Kola: You see that is my problem with you.
How did I fit into this now?

Tolu: You don't know for sure what you are getting yourself into, when you go about chasing females, would you?

Kola: Hmm, please let's just go and do what we came here for.

Tolu: Good, but remember, there are Spirits.
(This time trying to tease him)
In fact, I will do anything to make you stop this madness of yours.

Kola: When you see normal things, you call it madness. Are you any body's guardian?

Tolu: It is enough, let's just go.

Act Two, Scene Three

(Drumming began and the narrator was seen saying) The tales of place of Primary Assignment as I earlier pointed out hmm... in one hell of a process that seems rosy, tough, dogged within the ambience of our cultural sensibility. Indeed, man makes money but money rules the principle of a man. A hut covered with palm front is seen at the other end of the stage indicating a local drinking joint with Kola and Tolu alongside some villagers appreciating the beauty of the Maya (Maya is a drink).

Kola: Can I please get a chill beer **(***local favourite is the Hero beer)*

Tolu: Can I have a cold soft drink please?

(A quick drumming ends and the narrator is heard saying) The owner is seen from the other half of the Bar trying to bid his customers to come in while trying to attend to other things in person, as is the nature of the business.

Mr Coldliver: Hi Corpers, you guys must be new.

Kola: Yes sir.

Tolu: Hmm and how do you know this?

Mr Coldliver: Hmm, there is hardly any new person here in this village I don't know, Let alone Corpers. They have a way of looking around. (*And it smells fishy)*

Tolu: Wow, tell us, has any of those past Corpers ever done anything wrong?

Mr Coldliver: Hmm, well, some have done wrong, others were almost killed or at least we thought they were. *(Light find the narrator and he quickly opines that) at the mention of the word wrong, Kola loses his appetite because of his Intentions... please don't go nowhere)*

Tolu: Please Mr Coldliver continue, we need this.

Mr Coldliver: Well, strange things tend to happen in this village from time to time. You see during the Cashew season, one is allowed eating Cashew from any of its trees, but not allowed to go away with the seed.

Strange things will happen to whosoever goes away with the seeds. Again, do you also know that, there are many mad persons around? That is because it is pretty easy for people to make others go mad once provoked... And very few people escape madness once cast.

Tolu: Hmm, but how do all these happen?

Mr Coldliver: It's not how, but why they happen. You see, people don't take offence likely. Same way they don't take money issues likely too. That is why the town is called Oleagyida meaning home of sense **(***to be Smart)*

Tolu: I see.

Mr Coldliver; Long time ago a trailer crashed into the only major Bar we used to have in this village. Many say the gods are angry with the owner of the place. The vehicle cleared everything in its part including the owner's body leaving it scattered everywhere.

Tolu: Oh my God!!

Mr Coldliver: Corpers used to spend most of their time there. But they were not there that very day and only God knows why. However, all that died that day died mysteriously.

Narrator: *(Quickly appears and input)* indeed it is sad, isn't it?

Mr Coldliver; The people of this village can be rugged, if you mess around with them; you will get it from them and vice versa.

Tolu: Tell that to that my friend **(pointing at Kola)**

Mr Coldliver: Like one time, a Corps member impregnated a thirteen years old school girl and he was forced to marry the girl.

Tolu: Woo, that is good. Yes, good for him. That is the part I want to hear.

Kola: But...but what if he runs away before anyone knows?

Mr Coldliver: well, you don't know anything yet. You see all those churchy people? They all harbour shrines around.

Kola: Shrine my foot. That guy wasn't smart enough, "jor"

Mr Coldliver: See this boy o... you should fear. They said if the culprit runs, they will invoke the gods and he will himself become pregnant. I mean the belle will transfer to him.

Tolu: What! That is impossible. Haba Mr. Coldliver, what you just said is the most impossible thing on earth.

Kola: Well, you heard him. Hear these lies for yourself. Well let's just go home. I am done with my drink (whispers into Tolu's ears)

Mr Coldliver: I am sure you guys don't believe me, but it is simple and usual not to. But then, can you guys explain to me how and why those events I told you about happened? Go round for yourselves and see if you can find anyone picking Cashew seeds or Ogbono that does not belong to them. What about those mysterious deaths and madness?

Tolu: Well, sir I can't explain, but I think I want all of these to be true with the hope that my friend will at least be scared for once and then learn to respect people's culture.

Kola: Forget that thing, respect my foot. I am waiting for them. Look, some laws are universal. How can you say a man will get pregnant or that a fruit can actually report that it was picked?

Act Two, Scene Four

(Narrator shows up at the stop of the drums) At the Lodge, it was like a tale by moonlight in the evening hours of the day, as Kola wonders in his thought, Tolu whispers and goes over what was said at the joint.

Tolu: Look Kola, it would be nice if you just mind your business in this village ok. It is just me and you, and I am responsible for you, just as you are to me.

Kola: Let it go ok. It's just a fairy tale; moreover, it has nothing to do with my life style after all I'm not from this village.

Tolu: Look bro, it concerns you. It's not about your life style but theirs. As long as it concerns their female

Children, it concerns them. I know you, when it comes to female issues, you just won't stop.

Kola: I don't follow kids now; plus, the girls I follow are old enough to think for themselves.

Tolu: My problem with you is that you use deception, rather than the truth to get what you want. I can guarantee you that most of the girls you follow are not mature and the mature ones fall because you almost cry begging for the thing and owing that you may be good at it, it may become difficult to let you go.

Kola: What is that supposed to mean?

Tolu: You claim to be a player, right?

Kola: Ok, assuming I was claiming that.

Tolu: Well, you actually don't say what you really want from them do you? Rather you lie and hide behind the concept of love, even at that, you don't say if it's the love for the cookie or love for her as a human being

Kola: What are you saying this boy: how else should it be done? You simply say what they want to hear, if they belief you fine. And where they don't you move on or apply another strategy.

Tolu: Just listen to yourself. Where is the honour of a player in that? In American movies, we know pimps for their simplicity of convincing mature women to do what they want. And I also know that you and your type in Nigeria and most part of the world don't enjoy been referred to as pimp. It is not really nice, that guys go out and condemn girls and claim that there are no wife materials to marry. Don't you know that it is these girls that become wives? Anyways, your idea works on prostitutes, doesn't it? Because I can see you were going to call her a prostitute, right?

Kola: (Cuts in) of cause, she is a prostitute.

Tolu: Very well, who then patronizes prostitutes? Who encourages it in the society and finally, why do you think that it still remains the oldest business in history? The answer is you, because of men like you. So, why don't you just for a prostitute then.

Kola: Nope, that is against God.

Tolu: Hmm... really. So, you know this, yet you treat them this way. Ok, what constitutes prostitution then?

Kola: What the persons involved do, I guess?

Tolu: What they do, not who they are right? Therefore, your act, which is the act of sleeping around with different girls without considering any consequential effects, is also an act of prostitution. And as such, is against God Prostituting over an innocent young girl who does not know or is not aware that you are actually a prostitute is not right; in fact, you dent the image of the profession by so doing.

Kola: Well...

Tolu: *(Cuts in)* well what?

Kola: It is not entirely true.

Tolu: Well, my friend just be careful.

Kola: Why don't you mind your business? Plus, they always have the choice of saying No, right?

Tolu: Really! Do they really have the right to resist? If that is the case, then they should therefore treat those goats that will not stop at the first no for an answer, like the goat that they are right. Would there be true peace? I even gathered from some boys like you that persistence pays right? Indeed, they have the right to say no. Look, don't go around breaking young girl's hearts, according to Michael Jackson.

(The drumming starts and stops and the narrator is seen saying) I hope you have had something to eat...Now the NYSC, yes, the scheme consists of three major segments which is the camping, primary assignment and the CDS (community development service). On every CDS day corps members are expected to perform some sort of services to the community and then are to be oriented and informed of the latest happening at the NYSC secretariat as well as the welfare of other corps members serving in other parts of the state and the entire country, and how mutual understanding can be achieved amidst corps members and their communities, just get something to eat for I will be back exit.

Tolu: So, the story at the last CDS was not enough, I suppose? The local government inspector was very clear about situations like the one we are discussing.

Kola: I beg, please those are just stories to scare people.

Tolu: ok, I have heard you.

Kola: How is it possible that the parent of the pregnant village girl could summon a corps member who had finished service all the way from his village back to place where he served? And that just like that, he didn't know how it all happened. He just happens to find himself back there begging. Look you can scare others not me.

Tolu: I don't expect you to be afraid actually, because your type never gets scared. You guys did the same thing at the camp. You never listen to what's been said at the meditation ground. In fact, while the orientation is ongoing, you act like you know it all, like no one can actually tell you what to do. You behave like you are brave, only for posting letters to break your hearts and you start crying. It's your type that spends money he did not work for on beers at the mammy market only to cry to mummy that you ran out of money. Listen I know I might not be able to affect your attitude now or today, but I'm sure that in the nearest future just when you are old enough, you will look back to today saying that, it is just that I was young then, and that I couldn't do that now.

Kola: Until then.

Act Two, Scene Five

(The narrator now dancing to the drum and seen saying) The whole process now seems like a disturbance in the face of the existence and being... though we carry the holy book that is bigger than that of prophet Moses and sing more than Don Moen. We sing and mountains shake with the name of Jesus in our mouth like the good morning we wish our neighbours... hmm okay I reserve my comment... (Winks to the audience as if with a target).

Kola: *(In his room he sits quiet to examine all that have been said to him)* How could he suggest that I am a fraud and even a prostitute? Is he not in this society of ours, where a man will be willing and seriously wanting to keep a wife only to fall into the hands of a gold digger? Yes, this same society of ours, where a man marries a young village girl who is yet to see the world and she gets to the city, then her mother sends for you asking you to come collect the little money you paid for her because she has found someone better fit to be her husband! Yes, in this same society of ours, a girl tells you yes, I will marry you, in fact you are the only one in my life, only to be married to another person. I think I am better off being the winner not the loser.

Act Three, Scene One

(The narrator is seen presupposing after the drums stop) the quest to prey on his young target continues ...did I hear you say a man got to be a man? Lost to the fang of deceit and now, the question is, when a man feeds on the naivety of a woman, what becomes of him? The path to the stream is cool and breezy with the birds singing their lovely choruses, so much like in the animated love movies and is seldom used by the male folks of the community to woo young girls, as it's their cultural inclination that all young girls must go to the stream and so teenagers are seen going and others coming, Kola is one of them.

Kola: Hello beautiful?

Uju: Hello, but do you call me that because you desire to woo me by all means or do you really think that am that beautiful?

Kola: *(Shaking his head)* No, no, no. Listen fine girl, I must confess that you are the most beautiful being in form of a girl that I have ever seen my whole life *(Crosses his chest)*

Uju: Hmm, really?

Kola: Please, please, just wait a minute. What exactly do you eat? I know your people eat plenty of green; we do the same in my place. But what exactly do you add to it?

Uju: You have said it all that is it.

Kola: But we eat similar meals in my place, yet our girls don't look like you *(trying to support his fact with his body language)*

Uju: What do mean by, look like me? How different am I?

Kola: Well, I don't mean to flatter you, but do you not look at yourself? Or do your friends not get jealous of you and tell you how remarkably beautiful you are? If I may further ask, how comes you look the way you are? Your hip like what is only obtainable in the movies and I am sure it is even fake in the movies. How come you have such moderate body, yet it's one to die for, and you had no surgery? So fresh, at least from what I can see. you are Perfectly made, and needs further exploration, how comes your hair, even though you had not applied relaxer on it, shines and even curls, am sure you glow at night. Look at your legs *(this time pointing at them and bending down to see them up close and personal)* so straight and at the ankle they are tiny and at the thigh area they are round and sexy? Come fine girl, you are so filled up; every part of your body is filled up? No space for bones, so healthy I feel like taking a bite.

Uju: What!! You will bite me; you eat people where you come from?

Kola: No, no, no, am just saying that is a figure of speech in English language.

Uju: Really, okay. I thought you were really going to take a bite off me.

Kola: Ujulistic, I really like you and will love to know you better?

Uju: Hmm, after all these words who will resist you?

Kola: No, you can't, all I ask is a chance to show you, my love. And I shall give thee the best care ever. I shall carry you around gently like a wedding cake. I will continue to be your irresistible.

Uju: I don't know what to say.

Kola: Just say yes, I do.

Uju: *(Blushing at this instance)* as if I'm marrying you? Master Kola!

Kola: Please just call me Kola, calling me master does not fit you my dear Ujulistic.

Uju: Ok, my dear Kola, I have to go now. I will see you later.

Kola: Does that mean yes?

Uju: See you later Kola.

Act Three, Scene Two

(The drums stops and the narrator is seen enumerating) The compound of Mazi Udeh is well arranged with the design of tree plants as if contracted to a specialist and to the other end a small hut and a stick standing beside it tied with red wrapper and a woman in her forties pounding.)

Kola: Good evening mummy.

Mama Uju: Yes son, good evening, how can I help you? *(She stares at him as well as applying caution not to be offensive)*

Kola: Yes ma, I am Corper Kola, and I'm here to see your daughter.

Mama Uju: Hmm, Corper, please do sit down *(She showed him to a small wooden stood)*

Kola: *(Adjusting himself to the seat)* Hmm, well-constructed.

Mama Uju: Yes, my son, we had it specially made.

Kola: I can see.

Mama Uju: Hmm, Corper you say you are here to see my Uju, please what is your understanding with her? By that I mean arrangement.

Kola: Mummy I suppose you are Uju's mother?

Mama Uju: Yes, my son.

Kola: Ok am here as friend of your daughter. My intension for her is good. In fact, I have the intension of taking her serious and when possible, make her more than just a friend.

Mama Uju: Hmm... Well, Uju is my daughter, and she is a good girl. Plus, she is just a little girl, she still has to further her education you know? How sure are you about being friends with her? We barely even know you...but the case with corpers is that after a while they tend to leave. You have to struggle after service. How then do you intend to take care of yourselves if and when you get married? You know I have to ask all of these questions in case your intentions here are not good.

Kola: Mummy, please don't be troubled. With little faith all will be fine. With him all things are possible.

Mama Uju: Hmm, I see you are a man of faith too. *(Quietly, Uju walks in)*

Uju: Good evening mother *(Kneeling briefly as usual with custom)*

Mama Uju: Oh, my daughter, welcome back.

Uju: (Shyly) Good evening master Kola

Narrator: *The path of good tidings coming to play for a fact, it felt good in exploring the unforeseen.*

Kola: *(Feeling fulfilled)* Welcome Uju, how are you today?

Uju: I am fine, thank you.

Mama Uju: So, you two have met?

Uju: Yes mama, on few occasions on my way to the stream.

Narrator: (Mrs Udeh was not particularly happy this time and it is obvious why, for in most cases she (Uju) does not get back on time as she spends time in the unknown).

Mrs Udeh: Let me give you two some space then.

Uju: Master, what brought you here, I never invited you? You could actually put me in deep trouble. This fun you are getting right now is because my father is not at home. You better not be here when he gets back.

Kola: Uju, please will you keep quiet for a moment and let me speak to you.

Uju: Ok.

Narrator: (just as the scale of the fish was about to be removed the unexpected happen. There is a footstep approaching the house).

Kola: Who is that?

Uju: Oh my God it's my father, he is back. Welcome papa. *(Mazi Udeh enters)*

Mazi Udeh: Well, done my daughter, how have you been?

(Uju is shivering as she is not really comfortable with Kola around at that moment not knowing what to do.)

Mazi Udeh: And who might you be, in my compound and well relaxed? ... *(His face looking hostile)*

Narrator: *(The challenge of Enekentioba... hmm)*

Kola: I am Kola, recently posted here for national service *(stammering)*

Mazi Udeh: Of course, I know what national service is, but what are you doing here at my house?

Kola: Like I earlier said, I am a serving corps member to this community

Mazi Udeh: (*Re-adjusting his seat, understood that the young man was getting uncomfortable)* Hmm ok, you are welcome Corper boy. So where are you from?

Kola: I am from the West sir, and I studied engineering.

Mazi Udeh; Hmm, interesting. So, do you have any interest in politics?

Kola: Actually sir, I don't.

Narrator; *Mazi Udeh is a well-travelled man. He knows almost every part of the country that explains his interest in politics.*

Mazi Udeh: Well, my son that is the problem with you children of nowadays. You don't follow up with the trends of the land. Anyways, why are you here tonight?

Kola: I am kind of interested in your daughter.

Mazi Udeh: Did you just say kind of?

(Uju excuses herself at this juncture)

Kola: I mean I am...

Mazi Udeh*: (Cuts in)* Look young man, marriage and relationships are serious business here. I know that people from over there, have significantly gone a little soft about it, as a result of the high standard of social life there. We hear rumours of young people impregnating landlord's children and then becoming land lords them self. In the Benue, we hear of men who could offer any of their wives to visitors. In Calabar, the girls could follow a man once the love is there. While right here, the girls go after whosoever can spend money on them. Look young man I don't mean to unleash the mean side of myself on you. However, whatsoever your plans are here in this village, you should know that you will not get away with anything you do wrong. Is that clear?

Kola: *(Shaking his head in affirmation)*
Yes sir, yes sir.

Mazi Udeh: Hmm, well as for young and confident men like yourself, two things are certain, one you either stay or leave.

But remember that you cannot put something on nothing and expect it to stand. If you only want friendship from my daughter, please do let us know. If otherwise, also do state it. It will be unwise to deceive parents you know.

After I got married to Uju's mother and we grew older together, I discovered that there is nothing in it. I mean, in the hit and run business.

(The sounds of drums stop, and the narrator is seen explicitly saying) it's too early you say right? But the writing is visible and you might be wondering "why marriage" the idea is simple, young village girls are over protected especially from the social factor of the urban

area, so the logic is to get them involved as soon as the opportunity presents itself. And Kola might be one of those to involve.

Kola: Mazi Udeh no... That is not my intension... No, I will never do such a thing to your daughter sir.

Mazi Udeh: Very well boy *(rises to his feet as he bid him farewell, Uju walks in).*

Kola: *(Feeling relieved at this point)* Baby, Ujulistic Uju.

Uju: Baby? I am not a baby. And what is Ujulistic? *(As she steps forward to him)*

Kola: Can't you at least see that am serious about us, or at least taking us seriously? Look, I am in your house and talking to your parent. You at least believe me now, right?

Uju: Believe what?

Kola: That I love you, or else why would I want to be here?

Uju: Hmm, you have succeeded in getting me into trouble, now I'm not sure what you want and why me?

Kola: No, Ujulistic, how many times have I proffered my love to you, more so, what else do you want from me?

Uju: Master Kola, it's getting late, maybe it's time you take your leave. Should I get you something to eat before you go?

Kola: Hah, I know you like me, otherwise why do you show concern? Well, don't worry. I shall leave now. See you tomorrow then. *(He hurried away before the going gets tough).*

Uju: Ok master, see you then, I didn't say I like you... I just wanted to be good since you are our visitor. **(He is long gone**)

(In his mind, he felt yes, yes, this is it. The next time, hit, hit and hit.)

Act Three, Scene Three

(The drums stop, narrator appears to imply thoughts) in his room back in the lodge he feels great about the success of the day and tries to relay it to his cohort in the field of womanizing on the social media (whatsapp) they lay on a separate bed on stage, head facing each other typing on their phones and saying aloud...

Kola: Musty, what is happening? *(Typing on his mobile phone)*

Musa: My brother Kolawole, nothing much.

Kola: How are you doing? (*Speaking Yoruba)*

Musa: I am good my friend, how service area? *(Musa is a highly social guy who has spent time in the west, and understood the slang).*

Kola: Good bother, in fact I am very well.

Musa: I trust you, I am sure you have started doing your thing over there as a sharp guy.

Kola: Trust your boy, that is exactly what I am about to gist you.

Musa: Thank you bad boy, a player and an attacker with mad skills. If I were there, I have assisted you.

Kola: Anyways, do you remember my friend Tolu?

Musa: Tolu... yea Tolu, ok, I remember, that guy with crazy ideas right, what about him?

Kola: You got it, well we are actually serving together and he is killing me here with an even improved theory.

Musa: Ignore him, just why would he be urging one to do the impossible?

Kola: Imagine, he is saying dating a girl and having sex with her and then letting go is fraudulent.

Musa: Haha, what is fraudulent about it? They knew what was going to happen anyways.

Kola: Hmm, I told him exactly what you just said.

Musa: Does he mean that we should never date girls again or what? Maybe he wants us to just get married without making choices. Look, it's only normal what you are doing.

Act Three, Scene Four

(A sudden stop of the drums, narrator delves in, inputs further) Few minutes later, after his communication with Musa his friend in the act, he dashes into Tolu's room to mock him as well as to tell the Uju and her family visitation success story ...

Tolu: What is it and where have you been since?

Kola: You see! Musa and I just finished chatting and as a true friend, he did not mention anything like death, madness and so on. He also helped in debunking those crazy theories of yours.

Tolu: Which Musa, don't tell me, it's that spoilt friend of yours who does not behave like a northern person because he has been baptized into your cult of deception and conceptualization of social life. Please forget that boy.

Kola: Tolu what is wrong with you, you keep going on and on with huge grammars and non-make sense. It is called wooing. Guys do it and its cool and girls like it. If they fall for it fine none of my business. And I want to believe it is known as mutual understanding.

Tolu: Really, mutual understanding indeed. When, how and where is the contract of understanding, that you will woo her, sleep with her *(in most case, loose her virginity to you and the promise of getting married to her if she allows you)* then you make a U turn and tell her it's over in writing?

Kola: You have started right, making me look bad will not make what you are saying right you know.

Tolu: Look my friend, if you are dealing with a prostitute, it's a different issue and it's understandable. In fact, that is mutual understanding. Reasons being that, time and amount will be given to you and after that there is no bargaining. She would even ask if you are satisfied with the services rendered.

Kola: Ok fine. What will you say about girls who actually want it and she start throwing passes at you?

Tolu: That is an abnormal situation you know that right, given the kind of society we live in. The ladies don't often or are not literally permitted to behave this way. But where it happens, the unusualness should alert you, you may thus choose on how to treat her. More so, the ladies don't go that low in making their feelings obvious. A normal male, will treat her with respect and where he loves her in return that is fine. If otherwise, he should just let her know that, he feels nothing for her. However, the reverse is the case. Most males would consider if she is manageable. If yes, they will consider her approach and then pay back her love with the common phrase "you came to me, I never said I love you"

Kola: Hmm, your work!

Tolu: Seriously, you feel careless for their feelings, when a girl does that right? I mean approach you. But the situation is not the same with the boys making the passes and she sees it and makes a return pass at him. She may wish not to return pass. Apart from those in the prostitution business, normally girls don't do that *(walk up to a guy and make her romance intention known)*

It has to do with pride not money. Care, love, romance and most especially marriage, constitutes what a reasonable lady wants. But don't forget to properly classify the confused girls who may want all that I have made mention of but, may become confused later in a relationship due to the fact they may later be out of love. Now don't get me wrong, she is still not classified into the normal category.

(Please the word confused is used here not as an insult but to state an actual situation of being unable to make choice or indecision).

Kola: Now this is what I am talking about. You see yourself. So, the girls have the right to fall out of love *(not to be in love)?* If it's the boys that, did it, you especially, will be the first to call one fraud right? Look reasonable or not, they are all the same.

Tolu: Look Kola; in most cases such girls are too young to be in a relationship in the first place. Plus, the boy who was dumped is that one who may have lured her into the relationship. Most deformed men do it. I call them deformed because; a man goes to woo a girl that he is 20 years older than. What good do you expect from a man who does not respect himself? If she was staying because of the money spent, she will soon realize it and would want to quit. Other girls' wants strong men and they may have made it clear to the man but, he would insist that he would meet up and consistently fail. There are different real reasons why a genuine lady would leave a man. However, the reverse is the case with most boys. They will go for the most beautiful girl in the area and still get fed up once they are done using her.

Kola: Who then protects the man?

Tolu: Fortunately for you and I, men have always been protected in our society through our norms and values, and this is done so that, the woman does not become the ruler or head of the family someday. It is called patriarchal system of family. Finally, Mr Kola, no religious book permits the art of wooing in the manner in which it's done these days. And where courtship is allowed and mentioned, "no" sex is the order of the day. And this is what kills lots of the sex starved boys in courtship.

Kola: Well, my friend Tolu, if you like cry your eyes out. I don't care about all that you have said. *(Leaves Tolu's room in anger without the normal good night.)*

(Drumming stops, narrator appears, attempts to postulate) just when it seems everything has fallen in place the bell of be 'warned' is felt again... oh! my oh my, how are the mighty fallen. Few hours later in his room a seldom furnished one with his wall hanger to the left of his mattress and a stereo set. Chatting continues.

Musa: (Chatting) Hi, you are back?

Kola: Yes, my brother *(weakened by the words of Tolu)* brother, that guy want to kill me with his defence for girls. In fact, we had a long discussion not too long.

Musa: Look my guy; forget that guy and gist me what happen with you.

Kola: Ok then, there is this girl, her name is Uju. I call her Ujulistic. Men!! Guy, come see babe like angel. She is so fine I want to eat her raw. She is my newest catch brother.

Musa: I trust you, my brother. You don't waste time at all. Hmm... lovely girl, how does she taste like?

Kola: Calm down my friend, I haven't done anything with her yet, but it is a matter of time. I am done with the first phase though.

Musa: Ok then, take good care of yourself ok.

Kola: Ok and you too. Good bye.

Musa: Bye.

Act Three, Scene Five

(The drums start and slowly stops, narrator appears to cast the news) days go by and the message in form of a smoke comes forth from the east, the sound of victory, is it? Haha, the story of fulfilment, hmm... the story of mother and child in her prime...remember dear young and venerable teenage girls it's not victory, if it looks like what is about to happen (he laughs out of the spot and action returns to Kola's room).

Uju: Good evening master Kola.

Kola: *(Astonished, he makes to say a word but shuts up in the face of the unexpected visitation, then spoke)* Hey Ujulistic Uju, good evening, how are you? Uju, what brings you here, more so, how did you know I stay here?

Uju: Hope I did not interrupt anything? If yes, please don't be offended, I will take my leave right now.

Kola: **(***She is using his language on him he thought and if he doesn't do something fast, he will end up in regrets)* No!!! You came at the right time, in fact good timing, please come in. I shall fetch you some soft drink.

Uju: Don't worry master Kola, I shall take my leave now, after all I came just to say hi, since you were so kind to visit me last time. Paying you a return visit is the only thing I can do.

Kola: Good then, the more reason why you should come in. In fact, I insist you come in else, I will assume you did not come for me. When I visited you, I sat down for some time, but you will just leave as soon as you get here.

Uju: Please master Kola; I did not inform anyone at home that I will take this long or that I will be visiting a boy, so maybe some other time.

Kola: So, you still would not come in even for just a minute. Just a minute and you be on your way.

Hmm the feast of redemption (a voice from the back stage) Uju settles down to a bottle of Malt served by her host after due consideration.

Kola: I like your hair style; it makes your forehead glow and that is so beautiful.

Uju: *(Smiles)* Thank you, you are very observant I must say.

Kola: *(Draws closer to her this time)* what kind of cream do you apply on your skin?

Uju: Cream! I don't use modern cream. Just apply some palm kernel oil.

Kola: Hmm, see how they shine especially this area (*This time pointing at her thighs)* can I touch?

Uju: Touch what?

Kola: There, where it glows.

Uju: Just here *(Pointing at the thighs)* ok then. I don't know what is so special about my thighs.

Kola: Don't worry, they look beautiful. I think they are the most beautiful sets of thighs I have ever seen.

Uju: Well, I am sure you are just flattering me.You must have fine ones in the big city.

Kola: Oh Uju, you are not me, how then can you understand what I am saying. What my eyes see, I say.

Narrator: (Appears just to say) indeed when a dog is about to eat, it loses his sense of reasoning.

Uju: Ok, if you say so.

Kola: Uju if only you can look at yourself from the back, you are so beautifully carved. You have the curviest waist I have ever seen, from where the wrapper covering your soft spots *(the area around the chest)* to your hips. You have a beautiful belly button and your belly so flat too. Can I please touch?

Uju: It is just a belly and I wonder why it is so important that you touch all these parts you like.

Kola: They are so wonderfully made. The design is what amazes me the most. So fresh, so fine, it is only imaginable.

Uju: Kola, Kola *(she calls out silently) your* touching tickles in a way I can't explain.

Kola: Yes, I know I am also feeling the same.

(Narrator appears and is seen to be describing the scenario) He moves his palms round her body, oh! this part can't be said. Speak of confusion and naivety, oh speak of perplex and handicap. This is what being in this position will cause you, oh! you young and clueless.

Uju: Kola, *(she gently calls)* What are you doing to me?

Kola: Making you happy in love.

Uju: Is this how love is made?

Kola: Don't worry it will not hurt

Uju: Really, I was told otherwise?

Kola: Don't worry not thing will happen to you that you don't like.

Uju: Its touching like this I heard gets young girls like me pregnant.

Kola: Don't worry, I have a condom, it will protect you ok.

Uju: You should stop this please.

Kola: Don't worry it won't hurt.

Uju: I don't want it, please stop it. Wait, I also heard that all this is meant for the married couples?

Kola: Yes, but I love you and you know it, don't you?

Uju: Is love the same as marriage?
(Tensed at this point and confused)

Kola: Look Uju, people who are in love eventually gets married. And doing this is normal.

Uju: So, what you are saying is that, you are going to marry me?

Kola: Yes, yes, my dear Ujulistic. If I am going back to my place, I am taking you along with me if possible as my wife. *(Horridly just want to get started)*

Uju: Really!

Kola: Yes, my dear Uju *(nodding his head to the affirmative)*

Uju: But am I not too young for marriage, moreover, what about my education?

Kola: Girls not up to your age get married and still go to school with babies. Don't worry you will further your education.

Narrator explains as event takes place. He started touching her again, this time on her soft spots, she sat there watching the way he was carrying out his surgery, when it moves her, she will make some noise, it weakens her when he touches her there, thus, could not do anything, he continued until the deed was done, though it was her first time as it was painful, he was heated up and was sweating, he thought she look so beautiful and he had had his share.

Uju: Master Kola, I think I will be on my way. At least you would let me go now, right?

Kola: I wish I could keep you for some few more minutes but am sure your parent might be wondering where you might have gone to for this long. Take care of yourself ok.

Uju: Ok, I will *(paused to add a word or two)* master Kola, promise you will always love me, and will not let go, I am so convinced that, you will be the one, who put a smile on me. Remember your poems?

Kola: Cross my heart my dear Uju...

Narrator: Innocence and inexperience come with a price, many may say it's her fault, but in truth, many were victim before and still are. Though the mind is unwilling, but body is weak.

Act Four, Scene One

(Drums stops and narrator confidently confiding in the audience) a Butterfly cannot be a Bird for it must hearken to the smell of the pollen from the flowers and so it is, for it shall come in thousand folds. Thus, it's like men never change unless...let me sing a song of old....

The early memories
And sounds of music were
ringing round my
grandmother's door like
the locust plaque from the
East...

And so, it continued day after day, weeks and so on... boys will be boys, and men will be men. Steadfast in their attempt to break loose of any scenario they despise. Ask them, they dare deny it; it is in their nature to leave when they are done, especially if they have eaten it more than trice. The excuses are numerous. Most common being that she is not educated, her colour and sometimes her height is not enough. Mind you all of these were not taken into consideration at first. Furthermore, this is not to say that all girls feel the same about being cheated at, but even the toughest of them will be disappointed if this were to happen.

Uju: Knock, knock any one home?

Kola: *(Appears at the door and immediately said)* Uju listen, you have to stop coming at odd hours of the day like this, considering you were here yesterday. If anyone sees us, you might be in trouble. *(Swinging his face from east to west checking for passerby)*

Uju: What? Stop coming to see you, how? How can I ever stop? I don't even know how to stop even if I try to. Moreover, me can't stop because it's now like the snuff elderly people can't do without. Please I will just have to be careful.

Kola: I am trying my best here. Look Uju you don't have to do this. Please just stop coming for now ok. Let our gossips let go of us for now ok.

Uju: What gossip? I really don't get you. Who and where do you get this information from?

Kola: Fine, you leave me no choice, I wanted us to take things slowly but you will not listen, 'I don't ever want to see you again, and if you insist or persist then, you leave me with no choice than to disgrace you in front of this lodge, period.

Narrator

Uju's voice at this time brings Tolu out of his world to see to it that all is well...though not in the know of what has been on....

Tolu: And who might you be? Kola who is this and why is she screaming? Young girl what is the problem? Why are you here and why does it look like you are crying?

(She had drops of water coming out of her left eye)

Narrator: (Three things could be the bone of contention for her. One, the fact that she might have lost her dignity, secondly, her dream of getting married to a handsome educated Youth Corps member in future is about to crumble and finally what if the gossips did gossip and the winds emails it to her parents, her reputation in the village will be shattered. Yet in of all these, only the fact that he will let go of her that hurt her the most. Imagine that.)

Uju: *(Explaining to Tolu)* Master Kola has not been visiting like before, my father and mother has been worried. So, I came to check on him and the only thing he has to say is that, he is not one of our in-laws and that hurts because I thought he will make a good friend. But clearly, he is an animal.

(She turns and leaves, never to come back again, Tolu turns to Kola with an impression of disappointment).

Tolu: What have you done this time my friend? "I could curse you, you know", after all the warning I gave you, you still have been snacking a girl in this lodge without my knowledge.

Kola: Look Tolu, you heard her I didn't do anything; I only stopped going to see them that is all.

Tolu: I am sure she is just covering for you, plus she called you an animal that was an indirect accusation.

Act Four, Scene Two

(Drumming comes to a halt, narrator seen laughing and saying) Hulalahaha and so it went, as if the day will never bring forth the light of the sky but ladies and gentlemen sit back, relax for the journey is yet to be determined. Days gone by at the lodge, Tolu and Kola sits down under the large Ogbono tree to a basket of orange.

Kola: Tolu, I have wanted to ask your opinion on something.

Tolu: What is that?

Kola: What can you say about dreams?

Tolu: Dreams hmm, I think it's just a manifestation of the previous happening in the real world. I hope one of your girls is not hunting you in there?

Kola: Hmm hunt for where? Don't worry, I'm sure it's nothing.

Tolu: I am just teasing you; they are not real.

Kola: It's just that I keep on dreaming of losing my tooth. I mean they literally fall off one after the other.

Tolu: That is impossible in reality.

Kola: Whenever I get up, I feel pain.

Tolu: Don't worry; it's just your imagination.

Kola: Hmm.

(Drums halt at once, narrator seen dramatically foretelling) why will a dog eat a dog, why will the heart of man be as dark as the Coal tile road? For how long shall we stand and look? Indeed, the evil that men do lives with them and not after them... sound the gong. The hills and valleys bring around sometimes amongst the tall Ogbono and cherry trees some sort of chills towards evening hours. Lonely foot path and short cuts known as apian ways are often taken since it gives one time to commune with one's inner self, only this time, Kola communicated with someone or something else.

Spirit woman: Don't speak to yourself, because one may think that you have gone mad. Is that not what people say when you talk to yourself?

Kola: Who is that? Come out from where you are, you can't scare me!!!

Spirit woman: I shall not judge, because you don't do that either. But you and I are going to have a long-term relationship. What do you think?

Kola: Who are you and what makes you think I want to have a relationship with you, when I can't even see you?

Spirit woman: What if I can convince you to?

Kola: And you choose among the apian way to propose, you could as well say, that you want to behead me for ritual.

Spirit woman: I like you; I want to woo you. Let me promise you something.

Kola: And what might that be?

Spirit woman: You and I will have a happy ever after ending, and all your dreams will surely come true.

Kola: You don't even know me, and how can you give me all this without wanting something in return?

Spirit woman: Unlike you, this time, and unlike humans. I will tell you for now that I want something in return but only if you answer this riddle correctly. What hurts so real, so physical, so badly, yet reshape living, thinking and even destiny?

Kola: I'm sorry I don't have answer to that.

Spirit woman: Unlike you I will get mad at you. And you might even get punished.

Kola: What do you mean? Look I don't know who you think you are and what makes you think you have the right to punish me. Why don't you show yourself? Instead of hiding and making threats, why not come out?

Spirit woman: Your respect, young man or else.

Kola: Or else what, who are you and who do you think you are?

(Kola struck by a thunderous voice wave he unbelievably finds himself at a distance considerably far from where he was standing by the conjure of the spirit woman)

Kola: *(Coughing and stretching)*

Oh my God, what in hell is that?

Spirit woman: The next time I don't get a co-operation from you that is the hell that will reoccur to you, is that clear?

Kola: Ok, ok, just tell me, what do you want? (*Shielding his face from another attack).*

Spirit woman: The next few events in your life will aid you in at least responding to the riddle before you. Try to follow.

Kola: You still haven't said why you are doing this.

Spirit woman: Man by nature is a political animal. He strives to gain for himself to protect his interest first. He will never change from his ways unless, when in serious trouble. The moment his troubles are gone he will return to his old self. Man, only give when he is sure of receiving. He loves pleasure and despises pain. No man learns without pain only when the pain continues to torment him that he maintains the right path. So therefore, you will embark on a journey, I don't expect you to change completely, but you shall adjust and shall be able to determine why I am doing this to you. The answers are usually very visible, but only through a real lives event can they be revealed.

Kola: In case you think you can break me, cause me to start believing in spirits just like the people of this village do, you are joking **(putting up his feast, and squeezing it very hard)**

Spirit woman: You should take caution; else what happened before will re-occur.

(This time kola swallows his pride and maintains silence).

Spirit woman: During meditation at the orientation camp, what do you say? During sanitation, what do you do? Do you not turn against group decisions once it doesn't favour you? Do you not see young men and women who obey rules and regulations as scared and as children? Let's see how big a man you are. Shall we begin?

The light on the stage went off with horror like noise sound, signifying the treats to come.

Act Four, Scene Three

(Narrator appears, and this time seen story telling) one night, Kola falls asleep quickly only to see himself losing his tooth again, this time it's being replaced by one of the most hideous, horrible teeth he has ever seen, he was wearing the ugliest NYSC uniform ever. The cap is torn, the button ontop was sagging and dirty with black muddy stains he could barely breathe, yet it is hard, in fact it is as if it's a soldier's gadget at war. (The shirt (crested vest) is also torn and dirty and as hard as a bullet proof vest, his foot wear or jungle boot as it's called, same colour, and soul but this time as hard as a rock, its more or less like a corps soldier if I may put it that way. The conversion process is horribly painful because his hand and his entire body so strong and fit like he has been training and what is it about the old woman, he has been seeing her flashes. Kola wakes up panting as if been chased by a lion in a masquerade form with sweat all over his body with his mattress soaked as if bathed in a pool.

Kola: Tolu! Where are you, Tolu?

Tolu: Is it not too early for chat?

Kola: Please come out from your room or maybe I should just come in, it's important that I talk to someone.

Tolu: Don't worry me, be with you in a moment.

(Tolu comes out) Kola, you look horrible, what happen to you? You are sweating amidst this cool breeze of harmattan.

Kola: *(Chewing his words)* you remember that dream I talked about? I think I have become a full grown NYSC monster with bad, rusty horrible iron tooth.

Tolu: Kola, apart from the fact that you look horrible due to lack of some good sleep, I think you are ok. At least your teeth are complete. It must be your imagination again.

Kola: Will you just listen to me! A woman has been flashing in the whole thing, it's as if I can see her speaking but I don't know what she is saying. She has this very beautiful body but a very ugly head.

Tolu: Look Kola, just stop and I mean it, stop!!! You are still talking about beautiful even now that you look like this. What is wrong with you, why are losing your cool?

Kola: Why won't I lose my cool, you said it was just a dream, now am seeing things that feel almost real.

Tolu: Calm down ok, just calm down.

Kola: Look Tolu, the next time, you tell me to calm without saying anything reasonable, there is going to be a fight between us.

Tolu: Wow, listen to yourself, you are beefing me now, where is your bad friend Musa! Why don't you run to him?

Kola: Hmm, I don't blame you, if not for the fact that I'm used to you by now, why would I bring my troubles to you in the first place.

Tolu: Fine! After all I warned you about girls, and now you started doing old women too. She will kill you here, I am out of here!

Kola: Tolu! I am sorry, please come back.

Act Four, Scene Four

(Light spots the narrator, drums stops and he is seen enumerating) the night has now turned into the chthonic realm, the gulf of transition hmm, if only wishes were horses... the amalgamation of the latter and the former is now visible to the blind and audible to the deaf. Day is gone by and at night hmm, sleeping becomes difficult, maybe because of the unforeseen. Wishes have now become the order of the day, as Kola has turned a volunteered watchman who can remain awake all through the night. This time she appears. I have a mission for you she says, from now henceforth; this will be your routine. She then orders his transformation. Before his transformation starts, it was the first time the whole thing becomes visible to his eyes. And she spoke, she said, go to Lagos state, there is a Corps member like the former you. Go there and teach him a lesson, teach him not to mess around with young girl's heart and off he went. He disappears and reappears in Lagos state for real, it was on one of those streets in Lagos, he wakes up sweating after the events there and it dawned on him, and already awake, he yelled and Tolu came running.

Tolu: **(***Dashes in)* Kola! Where are you, what is the matter, why are you yelling?

Kola: Tolu! Please help me I can't move any part of my body except my mouth.

Tolu: Where are you?

Kola: Don't tell me you can't see me too. I am lying down here at this corner in my monster body. I told you about these dreams, it is going to kill me one of these days.

Tolu: Hmm, I can only hear your voice but could not find you. This room of yours is too dark.

Kola: It is not, my friend, I was lying right here in my monster body.

Tolu: Are you kidding me, what monster body are you talking about? And why were you shouting that loud?

Kola: What do you think I have been saying to you all along? I said my dreams are going to kill me one of these days.

Tolu: Just get up and take care of yourself. I will make you breakfast.

(Few hours later after breakfast, they sit to a discussion, as if he is going to listen to what Tolu has to say.)

Tolu: My friend, what is the matter with you these days? You don't go to teach again and every morning you wake up complaining of dreams. Look if you are not interested in teaching, please you can let the local government inspector know.

Kola: *(Lost in thought before regaining himself)* Look Tolu, you are still not listening to me; I am going through hell right now, why can't you understand? Teaching is something I have been doing for quite some time now and it isn't the problem ok. I seriously need help.

Tolu: Yes, you need help; it's high time you get yourself another girl to bully around in the name of love, right?

Kola: Hmm, you are such a fake friend

Tolu: Really, I don't hear you rejecting that.
You will always be you. The only thing you do with all your heart is chasing young girls around, isn't it?

Kola: Tolu just leave me alone; it seems you don't have anything better to say.

(Narrator is seen describing) Body ache, tiredness and serious confusion is the state he finds himself now, what to do, maybe he should just bluntly reject her in the name of God, or he should just drink Nescafe and remain awake, oh God help me (he screams in his thought) , it was night again, and as if he knew, that he couldn't remember what happen in Lagos, she appeared and said, your incompleteness of yesterday's task means you will have to go back today, this time all she need is the shadow of the night to appear and hunting starts, puff he appears in Lagos and this corps member is about putting finishing touches on his plan to chop and go.

Kola: Oh my God, Lagos for real, oh this is actually Lagos. *(The young man came passing, he didn't even know him until he heard him telling same thing he said to Uju. So, he waited for him to finish his rubbish, so these words are now sounding like rubbish to him now, but of because he is only but a monster that is on a mission. There he was in the shadows waiting, as soon as he is done, he appears before him)*

Kola: Young man! *(With a horrible voice)*

Corps boy: woo, what kind of ugly thing is this? Naa, it even has Corpers dress on.

Kola: Yeah! You better run for your life.

(The young corps member takes off, and runs until his legs could not carry him again and all he did was to appear before him, pinned him down and read out his faults)

Kola: *(Disappears and appears in front of him)* Young man, I have been sent here to teach you a lesson.

Corps boy: (Panting) what have I done to you and what lesson do you intend to teach me; please I don't want to die?

Kola: The following are your faults; you are about to fraudulently promise a girl you don't intend to keep your promise to. And you will always feel it is the only way of getting what you want if not stopped. You may even assume or presuppose that, that is how life works, whereas if that is how life work why don't you just quietly accept that the strong like me can do to you what am about to do right now and that is fair? I use to be like you, I have not even apologized yet. If you make it through this night, tell others ok.

Corps boy: Please and please, I promise to change tonight. This is it; I shall never do it again please I beg of you.

Narrator; (Is seen narrating) He wakes up in his room the next morning with the thought of his prey in his dream wondering if that will be his own fate as Tolu open his door)

Tolu: Kola! Kola! Are you there? Good morning, in case you are not coming to school, the principal said I should tell you to get well soon. I had to lie to him that you are not feeling too well, I am off to school.

Narrator: (Is seen pointing out thoughts) He calmly crawls out of bed, and came out for fresh air, in his words.

Kola: If only this boy will listen to what I have to say, but no, he only ends up criticizing me, these days my life begins only at night, I will just seat at home and wait for night fall, I have to find a way to convince this spirit woman this is bad and I can't be part of it anymore.

Act Four, Scene Five

Narrator: (Is seen pointing out facts) indeed the child that chooses to bite the fingers that fed him will be a guest at the house of bitter leaf soup. I need a song to quench my throat of thirst. However, Kola is in complete disarray and the way forward is yet unknown for the fear of the night is unprecedented.

Kola: (Lost in his thought) Night again, ok, where is she?

Spirit woman: (Appears) Young man! Stand-up it is time for another mission.

Kola: Look woman, I can't be doing this, am sure you are not real, go away in the name of God!

Spirit woman: In the name of God? Who do you think created all things good and evil? God knows yet, he allowed me treat you this way. Now get going, you will meet yourself at the mission ground, you know what to do.

Kola: Woman I am sorry to disappoint you, but I am not going anywhere. I can't be doing this for you. How am I sure you are even real? Please go away and leave me be.

Spirit woman: It is not your choice to make. You will do as I say whether you like it or not. And I will cut you lose when you complete your mission and provide answer to my riddle.

Kola: So, am on a mission, hmm, you call this mission? All I know is, this is bad, you are sending me against my will; I never agree to enter into any of this with you. This time around, I refuse to do as you have said, do your worst.

Spirit woman: Haha... **(She laughed horribly and it sounded almost the same as him when he is in that horrible body)**

(She conjured and he begins to change, he becomes, as horrible as before and totally not in control of his actions. It is as if he could hear himself talk, more like his thoughts, but could not control his body)

Kola: (Shouted) Am not your pet, please let me go, I can't be extinguishing people for you.

Spirit woman: Yes! Yes, you are Corperstein; you shall continue to extinguish those in the same attitude as you until they learn their lesson.

Kola: (Horribly speaking now) But fellow Corps members are to be secured by others at all cost that is what we are told at the camp.

Spirit woman: You should have thought about that before you and your kind of devourers embarked on your missions diluting young girls' blood with your bad Corper's blood. Listen, today's mission is in Calabar. I expect a fine job, and be careful, this one is strong!

Kola: And I have become your servant of war.

Spirit woman: Yes, war against indiscipline young male Corpers, now go.

Act Five, Scene One

Narrator: (Seen pointing out facts) in the place of a dominant power, the residual gives way and such is the existentialism of men. Exception in the otherwise certain future is such a waste of eventuality.

Kola: (He appears before the Corp boy in cross river in the face of his mission) Young man! Am here and your time here is over. Before I start, here are your faults.

Corp boy2: Who the hell are you? You ugly corps member!

Kola: Community Development Service (CDS) is not an avenue for you to introduce young girls into the immoral act. Your plan to let her in on the real deal tomorrow will end today. More so, if I don't stop you now, you know, I may never stop myself. Today you lay to rest this style of yours.

Corp boy2: You lie, you ugly beast. Today we die here together!!

Narrator: (Seen describing the events) as he rushes towards him, he pulled out a machete, only God knows how he had it all along. So the fighting started. He was tough. It took a while to bring him down to his kneel. And only then did he realize why he was constructed that way. That the hat so strong is for protection so that he doesn't get to break his head, even though it was hideous. The khaki top was also designed to serve as a body armour, it protected him from all the hit. The jungle boot was also handy. As they fight into rough land Kola definitely needed protection for his feet. The question he should be asking is why all this? But the answer is already known. It is so as to be alive, suffer humiliation due to his hideousness and the same time to get the job done. Well, eventually the Corp boy started to beg. I am sure he has taken enough heat, he had smashed his legs. He is strong, but probably from drugs.

Corp boy2: Please! Please! I give up, I confess. Please forgive me, I promise never to do that which I have planned to do tonight. Please have mercy.

(Both panting heavily, at this time)

Kola: Am sorry I cannot spear you, I have to finish what I have started.

Corp boy2: Please I beg you once more, who asked you to do this to me, have I ever wronged you personally?

Narrator: (stating the point) he is trying not to do this, but the body is not controlled by the mind. More so, the essence of this is not personal but a divergent disassociation formula. You will get it in the end.

Kola: (Assert) young man, I have told you, I can't help you right now. Even if I wanted to, I usually can't. I was sent to do this.

Corp boy2: Ok, but at least tell me who sent you and what did you do to deserve this? **(What to know why kola looks like that)**

Kola: Well exactly what I did to deserve all this I don't know, but I was told you did behave like me so, I have to extinguish you. As for my looks, the woman who sent me did this to me.

(Drumming stops follow by the final action, narrator seen explaining the action) Just before the end of that statement, smash! Smash! And smash on the young man's head and the next thing that happened to Kola was that he was back home struggling to find his bearing and to transform into his normal self, you can guess the horror.

Act Five, Scene Two

(Drumming starts and stops, orator seen, stating the aftermath) The morning after the adventure to the land of the unspeakable, the event is becoming normal, so there is no much panic, but the concern remains great and the need for solution and cause continue to get attention from Kola, plus he just needed to ask someone for help, Tolu is only helpful in discussing theories, wants to know about dreams, he has to find out elsewhere.

Kola: Tolu! Tolu! Where are you? Good morning.

(Tolu sluggishly appeared at the door step)

Tolu: This boy, what do you want this morning? More so, your night was relatively quiet I must say, no more dreams, right?

Kola: Exactly, why I am here this morning.

Hope you are not going to bore me with those crazy concepts of yours.

Tolu: Thanks for the insult this morning, if I may, please what is it that you want from me this morning?

Kola: Ok, it is good that you didn't notice anything strange from me last night, but

I need to know more about dreams?

Tolu: Well, like I said before, dreams are the manifestation of your previous participation in a past occurrence.

Kola: Ok doc, what can you say about my being in Calabar yesterday's night?

Tolu: What! You have started again, right?

Kola: Look young man I am here because this matter is as important as my life is to me. I am not kidding at all.

Tolu: Hmm, **(shakes his head in pity)** you have finally lost it, how is it possible to even be in Calabar just this morning and still be here now. Well did you go by plane then or maybe it is in a Ferrari car?

Do you even know how many hours it takes to get Calabar and back here?

Kola: Young man, forget all that crap, please I need help, because I was just coming from Calabar this morning and I can't really tell if it was a just a dream or it is for real.

Tolu: Ok, if you wish, maybe should go and see a psychologist. Oh! We are right in the middle of a village where there is no psychologist.

Look I want to help you, but where do we start from?

Kola: Psychologist for what? Did I say I was going mad? I only wanted to ask someone who knows anything about this.

Tolu: Ok, like whom?

Kola: what about the likes of Mr Coldliver.

He should be able to help or at least recommend someone who can.

Tolu: Ok settled then. But don't you think it's too early to go and see him.

Kola: Come on let's go. It's urgent.

At Five, Scene Three
(At Mister Coldliver's Shop)

(Pam Pam, drumming stops, narrator seen educating) mostly found in most suburbs or villages are people like Mr Coldliver. They usually own a shop as it's called or let's say a hangout spot where people from urban areas chill out to drink and eat fried meat and roasted fish. It also provides avenue for the city people to meet with the locals. Did you also know that this is where one can get the latest gist?

Kola: Pkam, Pkam, Pkam

Mr Coldliver: It's a shop, you don't have to knock you know.

(A few moments later, after much explanation)

Kola: So, Mr Coldliver that is my story.

Mr Coldliver: Well, my friend, I have heard you. But you see. Remember what I told you before.

The village is strange, but actually no one has ever had answers to most of these things happening. All I

can say is that, your dreams could be that your body or spirit is not in agreement with this place.
Have you considered relocating?

Tolu: We are with the corps; relocating is not really up to us. Not even now that we have all settled down in our various places of primary assignments.

Mr Coldliver: Well, I really can't help you guys. I don't even know where to start from.

Kola: Ok Mr Coldliver, am very grateful for your support. Have a pleasant day sir.

(Both left the shop)

Narrator: (seen pointing out thinking scenario) hmm, he wondered off in thought, and in his memorization, it occurred to him that people do behave this way, they will say they can't help you, and this is not because they really can't help, but because usually if something goes wrong in the process of helping out, they too will be held responsible for you, all right, now no one will help.

Tolu: (On their way to the lodge) Kola!
What is wrong with you? A young girl just past us by, and while you were at the front, she greeted you and you snubbed her.

Kola: Who cares who is greeting, this time is not the time to act as if all is well, it's not a movie you know.

Act Five, Scene Four

(This time, narrator appear behind curtains elaborating) Kola was under intense pressure, I must say, telling friends have not really solved his predicament, neither has pleading helped. Maybe he should rather focus on the problem which is himself he thought. At least that is what the woman has said. But what exactly has he done to her in particular. One of the young Corp boy asked him similar question and he was unable to give a sound answer as to some of the possible reasons why she has been asking him to take care of fellow corps members who have been into the game. He knows he is into women, and since he has been here, he has since been with just one girl and that was Uju. Hmm, could Uju be behind all this, could she be the woman who has been tormenting him? If she was, what did he do to her to deserve this? Can he just walk up to her and accuse her of this? What would people say and what prove does he have to defend himself. His instinctive thought to himself would be that, what if the things he does and the horrible words he used in deterring these girls are coming back to haunt him. He may have over done it this time. He assumes the girls understood what they are going into; like kola I too guess you the audience ought to understand what the girls in Kola's life were going into

when he told this one to stay off. Well only this time he may have chased away the solution to his problem and even if she is the problem, it is more of Yanga- dey- sleep- Trouble- go- wake am.

Kola: (He wakes up in one of those occasions asking) where am I and where is this place? (He has not been sleeping fine these days, his life begins at night these days, he has been to several mission, in most cases he has survived, but sometimes, he is badly hurt, other times he come back home unscratched.

He can't really say it has been a pleasure but he must say the reasons for his mission are beginning to have meaningful justification. However, the fighting is beginning to take its toll on him. He often comes back home tired and super weak. Most like crashing into his bed without knowing how he got home, especially if he had fought with the corps members with charm or who is in form of a cultist. This time around he appeared in Akwa Ibom State and his mission was a young corps member with spiritual powers)

Corps boy3: Haha, I felt your presence even before you appeared here. What do you want, you evil spirit?

Kola: (*Stood behind him and said)* your days as a champ have come to an end. Here are your faults.

Corps boy3: Shut your mouth, who are you to tell me where I have gone wrong? Look you have met your match today.

Narrator: (Still elaborating) the fighting starts, to Kola's greatest surprise he turned into a big black snake. And the next thing he did was to bite a passer-by hoping that kola would probably care for the person. Instead, kola went after him flogging him with his belt. After much struggle with him, he turns back towards the already bitten person who is already struggling for his life and this time bites some flesh off the person and went into his body. While he was going in, kola was flogging him. Kola was unable to stop him from going in. He eventually went in and the person who is supposed to be dead stood up and the fighting continued. He became very strong, much like the strength of ten men. It took a while but he eventually bows, but both lay lifeless, at the end kola was drained of energy. The job is done and on his way home kola crashes.

Act Five, Scene Five

(Lightening like that of thunderstorms and winds like hurricane, villagers seen running for their lives. It is the early hours of dawn; Kola comes out of nowhere crash lands in the middle of the road to the stream in the forest. Uju appears, even though she is afraid, only a Corper would look like that and she happen to know the only two Corpers in the village, she must take a look)

Uju: Hideous as it may look, but where did it **come** from? It looks injured and breathing heavily *(a sudden high breath and finally stops breathing and it face begin to appear clearly)* how could this be? (*Shifts backwards)* this cannot be, master Kola *(calls for help)* Help! Help! Someone please help me. (*Runs to the right and back to the left for help)* master Kola say something, talk to me please. What happen to you and why do you appear this way? What have you done to yourself? (*Calls out again for help)* master, master *(check quickly for pulse, but there is silence and stillness)* could he be dead? God forbid it, I could be saying the abominable. *(Covers her mouth and begin to cry)* Please don't, please am begging you.

(Silence and still he lay, this is it, and it is only a matter of time before it occurs, maybe not this way, but it is certain for those who harbour such life Style)

Uju: Even though my heart still aches, it pains me to see you go, for the little joy the little time we spent together brought forth. How sad it will be for your parent that you end your life here. You left without saying goodbye. Kola! Kola! Kola, come back, even if not for my sake, at least for the sake of those who cares to hear our story. And for those who are yet to hear your poems. How quick I forget, how soft my heart, no wonder it's taken for granted, but what shall I do. You cheated me, you cheated me master Kola, if you leave me this way. You cheated me.
(Heavy wind, spirit woman appears supposedly not seen, spoke to kola silently).

Kola: Help, help, somebody please help *(Crying out)*
Uju: Oh my God, you are alive, help me, somebody please help me
(Help eventually came and he is taken away)

Act Five, Scene Six

Narrator: (Describing a state of mind) (He) Kola begin to notice that he could open his eyes slowly, because he has been alive in his head, although could not move. He knew he was not going to be home because he actually knew that he crashed landed. Hum, hum, he tried to speak.

Kola: Who is here, and where am I, anyone please help? **(Speaking slowly)**

Tolu: Hey, take it easy chameleon, am here.

Kola: Tolu, oh it's you. Thank God, you found me.

Tolu: Yes, thank God, but no, I didn't. Actually, I was at home when a young girl came and requested that I come with her immediately that you were hurt. I got here and found you in bandages, and that you were actually found in the woods. So, I would love to ask you one question if I may.

Kola: Please do, unless if it is not about madness and psychiatric.

Tolu: How the hell did you get out of the lodge without knowing until found brutally injured and left for dead in the road I know you have never been to?

Kola: Hmm, where do I begin now? First, I would like to say that, I have been trying to tell you this for a while now but, you don't listen!!! Secondly, I crash landed on my way from a mission. The corps boy was so strong and corny too, very manipulative I must say. My friend it has been very horrible for me and I have sort help in all possible means, but no cure, not even from you Mr Theorist friend.

Mama Uju: (Knock, knock) thank God you are awake, my husband, you said it; he is awake, **(its mama Uju calling her husband)**

Papa Uju: Yes, I knew he was going to wake up. I also know you did a nice job because you are the best at adjusting bones in this village.

Mama Uju: Thank you my husband, kola. How are you doing?

Kola: Mummy I am fine, thank you ma. Permit me to say, that I was highly surprised at seeing you people before me. I have been at your house before but I only had the chance to seat outside. This is probably the inner part of the house, and am I actually inside your home? **(Surprised to see the very people he might have been hurting shortly after speaking to her, Uju walks in and the mother left)**

Uju: Thank God you are getting better.

Kola: Yes **(Speaking slowly)** I guess I don't have to ask how you are here after all it's your house.

Uju: Am sorry, if I have offended you, I only wanted to find out if you are getting better.

Kola: Offence nope, like I said it's your house. But I suspected you, and how did I get here in the first place? Am sure you brought me here to finish me right, go ahead then finish me, do it right now, do it!!! **(Struggling to get up)**

Tolu: Kola, take it easy will you, you can't even move. Kola... I say wait a minute,

(Trying to calm him down) you can't even move any part of your body, can you? Yet you want to attack her, what is wrong with him please **(asking Uju).**

Kola: Why are you asking her, what can she do? Moreover, she hasn't answered me yet, how did I get to your house? I'm sure this is your room, right?

Furthermore, what are your parents doing to me? Oh, just maybe they knew they knew what has been happening to me; you all connived in doing this right, answer me? If I could get up, I will strangle you myself.

Tolu: Kola, will you please shout up for once, am trying to find out exactly what is going on here.

Kola: And does it look like you are asking a doctor, or you have gone mad? Please get me out of here; I need to go to the hospital right now!!!

(Tolu and Uju both shouted, shout up!!!)

Uju: I think you are experiencing nerve damage. **(She turned facing Kola)** I was on my way to the stream as usual when I found you, carrying you was so scary because, for every place we laid our hands, you will scream. The worst is that I could hardly get help to carry you here. Because you were with some monster or like some monster, so scary such that it felt dangerous to even come close to you at the time, it took the intervention of some boys whom had been my friends right from child hood to bring you here. But one thing that surprises me is the fact that when we got here, none of those form remained. You were you again only that you were badly hurt. So, being that mother is a healer, I brought you here. It was in the process of putting back your broken bones that you screamed and passed out. Once again thank you for your kind appreciation.

Tolu: She is the young girl who came to inform me of your where about. You should learn to say thank you instead of blabbing about. More so, what does she have against you that would warrant you use such hash words on her. Look Uju am very grateful ok thanks a lot.

Narrator: (Describing a moment of sadness) she turns to leave and he began to cry, Tolu tried to pamper him but enough tears has come out of those eyes of his. The feeling is not pleasant I tell you. It could not be her at this moment he imagines. In fact, no one but Uju could help, because of the love she has for him. And he has offloaded all prospective accusations on her already. She reminds him of that day in his room, her innocence and naivety still reflected. Tolu's telling him it wasn't his fault and that all will be well soon wasn't good enough. But the tears that fell out of his eyes were not for his sake but for the selflessness that Uju had shown. She did to him what he honestly doesn't deserve. Should he say that since it is health matters, it's only fair that she does so? If he was to assume that this predicament was completely her fault in the first place, what is his role in it, and why would she and her entire house help out now? Did she also determine where he was to crash? If yes why not command that he crashes into the sea or into a highway or even a lion's den? I know some persons might say, so that he did be forced to confess. But even confession is for people who have been involved in a mess one way or another.

Kola: Uju! Wait a minute, am very sorry for everything I have said and may have done to you that hurt you. From the responds of mama, am sure you did not inform her about the problem between us, I was only carried away that is all.

Tolu: (Cuts in) what is the problem. Kola!
What have you done again even on the sick bed?

Kola: Don't you remember her? She is the young girl that was crying at the lodge some time ago who won't say exactly why.

Tolu: So, you did hurt her that day. I told you.
I always warned you but, you won't listen. Now she turns your Saviour. Had it been me, you will rot there. Kola, your action resembles that of a man who feels that it's rather absurd to wash the underwear of a woman **(wife)** whom he loves so much. And then use his mouth in the same area where the underwear is used. Men in our society claim of dominance over women nowadays have gotten out of hand. They simply forget that apart from some few instances that most women may take advantage of the situation to frequently demand that their man continue to do this, it's just underwear. You may even end up asking her to do same for you and that is not wrong right?

Uju: I didn't tell anyone because it was none of their business. Furthermore, my father would have hurt you before now, and still will if he finds out. Let's just pretend nothing happened between us in the past and we are good. You owe me nothing except, if you wish to give mama something. No hard feelings please get well soon bye.

Act Six, Scene One

Narrator: (no action here but a better understanding is possible just go through) She left them, and Tolu would not stop talking to him and he was not himself. Her mother walks in and spoke.

Mama Uju: You may not be able to walk or move any part of your body for now and my daughter may have to be the one to feed you, change your cloth, dispose of your excreta. And Tolu should go and fetch some of your clothes from the lodge.

Narrator: So, it was that he spent the remaining of the months of service at Uju's. Some time she would find it in her heart to say hello, other times, she would come for him only, and no fun, and no talking even though he did continue to plead with her. She gradually eased up and they got talking.

Uju: You are lazy, you complained when I touch you where it hurts.

Kola: But of course, it hurts even though in a sweet way.

Uju: You are good looking when you sleep, but the only thing that spoils you is the fact that you are a cheat, and ungrateful.

Narrator: He would also spend half of the whole day waiting for her to show her face even when it isn't time for her to come feed him or clean him. And when she does, he would always tell her of the fact that.

Kola: Uju you know that without you I did be dead by now. And I shall continue to be grateful to you. And anyone you finally decide to trust would be the luckiest of us all.

Narrator: During this period the woman did not visit, until she finally did the night, he was planning on telling her that he did love to go back to the lodge to continue healing. She told him why she did what she did. She spoke

Spirit woman: I am a spirit not evil, but often looking for who to possess along the apian way, when I had Uju's thought of how badly treated she had been, so I decided to show the person responsible, how it feels when he decides to use deceit. Because what he has done is not only deceitful but fraudulent. Hope you have learnt your lessons.

Kola: Lessons well thought and amazingly learnt thanks.

Narrator: Many months have passed. Now he remembers what the bike man on their way to the bank said, and what Mr Coldliver also said, the village is indeed strange. You know one of those moments you fall seriously ill and you think you are going to die? You say to yourself that death was imminent thus it was necessary that you make confession on a whole booklet to either ask for God's forgiveness or at least warn those upcoming law breakers that, life is actually very simple, if only they just take it slow. All of these moments gave him time to become ripen, just like the pawpaw fruit and ready to be eaten. Sometimes, just when it seems right, he goes visiting even though Uju's mother would complain that he was not fit enough to start walking the distance.

Act Six, Scene Two

Narrator: at the lodge a guest is expected.

Tolu: Did your friend musty call? He said he will be coming to visit you, when I told him what has been happening, he insisted that he needed to pay you a visit,

Kola: No, when is he arriving?

Tolu: Don't know maybe today, probably evening things.

Narrator: (seen saying) Tolu received a call and it was Musty, so he went to get him over to the lodge. When musty came, they took time to discuss and kola gist him all that has happened in recent times. He felt pity for him and consoled him with plenty of jokes; it was the one thing Tolu does not do. And in no time, he started to feel like his old self again. The confidence was coming back to him. And for once it was nice being alive and not disturbed by the facts that, once its night he would be disappearing again. Now, the one joke Musty didn't tell is the fact that, he doesn't do alone. He is always with a girl whether at home, in school or even when visiting a friend. And this time around, the victim is another innocent Uju from the village where he is serving. Only

God knows if she has parent, who ought to have restricted her movement, but that isn't the case. He is here with her. So, at first it was Tolu who did something or said something as the case may be.

Tolu: As usual right, your work! So, you have not change, you are still on this ugly way, right? **(Supposing his is a changed person).**

Musty: Kola, what is this unsocial friend of yours saying? Am not kola for your information, thus your words don't work on me you hear?

Kola: Guys, please stop it. Is it not enough that there is a girl in there, you stand out here and talk as if she doesn't exist? Ok, Musty blew it, yes, I know him, and I know what he is capable of doing but, this right here is just not fair. Maybe I am saying this because of the ugly experience of recent, but it hurt? I also know that some girls can be that daft that they see nothing wrong with boys saying awful things about them in their presence but, that should not be the case here?

Narrator: Uju came by

Musty: Kola you know these girls. They have cockroach brain. You know they are not wise at all. Many at times they think one is going to marry them as such, they claim to be making sacrifices. While some are just wasted and want to just enjoy life.

Kola: I understand what you mean.

Uju: Really! You side with all that he has just said? I should have known that you will never change. In fact, there is no change in you. You are still the old master I know, dubious and conniving in nature. My mother asked me to bring this to you **(Stretching him a cup of herbal mixture)** I don't want to ever see you again, and if I do, I will let everyone know of what transpired between us. Hope you understand what that means. The whole village, my father and his kinsmen, the school and your service are as good as over. You might even put innocent master Tolu in trouble thanks to you. And don't dare follow me.

Kola: (Shocked) I didn't mean it in that sense, don't think that way (trying to stop her), I was going to be fair to both parties. I meant Tolu is right, while Musty might also have the right to live his life the way he chooses.

POEM

Oh, what have I done?
Just when it was a fine tone,
And thy dance is thus done,
There has to be a stone,
But stones will always be there,
I was supposed to be elsewhere not here,
To repent and to backslide,
Is like the angel and the devil collide,
Now already broken can't chase her,
If I can, how far was thy willing to further,
Go thus far, get thus crushed, and go back forth,
Come thus near, lose thou crush, now thou caught,
To the old ways broken and this time even more,

To live or to correct these mistakes forever more.

Kola: Musty, I think it's time you live, and please discharge of that little girl of yours as you do so; it's for your own good. I wonder why I wasn't sent to you as at the time I was travelling.

Musty: What!! It's me o, its Musty you are throwing out of your lodge because of that thing. I'm sure that is the girl you were telling me about; I should have known she got you. And I'm afraid you messed up man.

Tolu: Musty you heard him, leave right now or else. (Speaks calmly)

Musty: Don't worry, I will leave right away, my only regret is that I thought I was visiting a true friend in the game.

Narrator: (Seen pointing at the distance) Kola went after her, after clarifying things with musty, but only God knows how it ends.

Act Six, Scene Three

Kola: So, dad, here I am, a changed man. Your son has become a theorist. Remember when I said something hit me, yes it was ideas. It has always been there. It's just that, I have never looked inward. And guess what, looking inward is actually rewarding. It gives you perspectives, you constantly want to solve problems and you see reason to always be a law-abiding citizen or corps member. Thus, the new look and the new me.

(And to Tolu, my dear friend and saviour) Tolu you have come to make me understand, that when men feel that they are clean, *(And of course this is the African man's mentality)* who then makes the women unclean? That if a woman is a prostitute what then do we call those who patronize prostitutes. When we are done with all none wives' materials where do we intend to find wife materials, plus who will manage the ones that we have rendered useless. And finally, I say unto us, that no amount of detergent will wash away the woman in the woman we eventually settle down with, and therefore she is a victim of the very act we commit now and call fun. Finally, this is not saying that science best explains these, but using factorial

methodology, by deducting every female in our mist the last one standing might just be our mother, or someone else's mother. In the end, PAIN is the answer to that riddle, it's the one thing that makes destiny what it's, pain because it hurts, and if its hurts you have learnt.

Kola's parent: *(Spoke at the same time)* so where is she?

Kola: She said to let her go, if it was true love.
I had to let go of her, because it turns out that it was true love after all.

Mr Alabi: My son (stirring at him with a facial
Expression that looks like he had pity him for quite some time now but relieved That he had become a man) There are two of everything (Phenomenon) in this world. While the first is the event proper, the other is the reciprocal result of the former. You may have never believed me if I had stood my ground that you must change in the past. Son let me educate you about sex. When you are young, your body speaks louder than your mind. So, you think every contrary advice against sex is crap. Studies have shown that the human brain can be manipulated with drugs, thus the man, can become a woman. Do you know how they did it?

Kola: No papa.

Mr Alabi: Well, this is because they understood how the brain works. The human brain could make something disgusting to one man the most interesting to another. If you are familiar with the concept of spirit over matter, you will as well understand that it's what the brain translates to you that seems real to you. Therefore, sex is an act of physically or imaginatively Interacting with an organ in the human body which has the tendency of causing stimulation when blood rush into it as commanded by the brain given the right atmosphere which is as a result of some metabolism external to the body to release reactionary substance, which then causes pleasure to the body. It's only human nature and can be manipulated I.e., using drugs and training the mind.

Kola: Hmm.

Mr Alabi: This is the only logical explanation as to why hormonal drugs are available. And it also explains masturbation, lesbianism, gays and straight. The fact remains that when the consequential fluids is released, an individual gets the satisfaction, which is only temporary. As such, if any of this is harmful to you, you have to stop by using the mind training strategy.

Kola: But dad, it's not as easy as you think.

Mr Alabi: I know, but mistakes like yours is often misunderstood for fun, whereas it hurts you and others involved **(the girls)** I just want to let you know that it's not spirit or a curse as people make it to be, you can control it, for instance waiting until marriage or abstinence.

Look the reason why people find it easier to change partners, switch or replace one is because they allow their brains to make them feel it's the real deal.

Mrs Alabi: my son, love involves care, respect, memories, feelings, responsibilities and demonstrating oneness with one's partner. Underline the word ''partner''

Curtains drop, spotlight appears on the narrator and he is seen saying, ladies and gentlemen, the school of thought that holds that man by nature is naturally wicked and selfish may have slot in a point here, but what we as men perceived as social justice is on the contrary. Thus, the assertion by another school of thought that man by nature is naturally good and selfless. We should dismiss this assertion and try not to forget to understand what it means. ''Most of what is just according to law is against nature and men who are not self-assertive loss more than they gain'' Antiphon

To say women are weak, inferior (a lesser being), unwise and indecisive, and are designed to be dominated by their opposite sex, the male, is to agree that, slavery, colonialism, neo-colonialism and imperialism against the black race and other enslaved people for many years by their white colonialists is not only right but justified"

Joseph David Ari

-The End-

FOOD FOR THOUGHT

What is life? Is it a way of living or simply just being alive? Whatever it is, you will notice that the actions you take in life are the only things that are real to us. But if you are not told this, you wouldn't know. Imagine not having eyes, how would you justify what you see. What will be the true nature of what you see? In case you are thinking about that statement, whatsoever you do that you feel is wrong, is bad, even if it seems right to others. Consequently, whatsoever you do, that has a negative impact on the lives of others is wrong. You will know by simply putting yourself in their position. Listen, nothing in life is real except these three things: Life, Death and God. If there is anything that takes Life, don't do it. If it causes Death, don't do it. Finally, remember that God alone has the power to do things and undo them.

Joseph David Ari

www.ingramcontent.com/pod-product-compliance
Lightning Source LLC
La Vergne TN
LVHW012113160826
845678LV00014B/3080

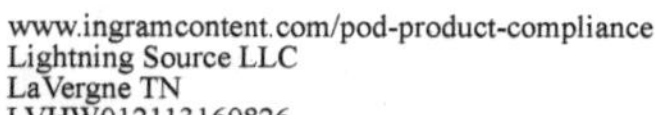

* 9 7 8 9 7 8 9 6 5 1 2 2 1 *